Adapted by Frank Berrios

Based on the teleplay "Beyond the Known Universe"
by Brandon Auman

Illustrated by Steve Lambe

 A GOLDEN BOOK · NEW YORK

T#: 465461
ISBN 978-1-101-93694-8
randomhousekids.com
Printed in the United States of America
10 9 8 7 6 5 4 3 2 1

While trying to save Earth from an evil race of aliens known as the Triceratons, the Teenage Mutant Ninja Turtles, April, and Casey found themselves aboard a spaceship—with a very strange Fugitoid robot.

"My name is Professor Zayton Honeycutt!" the robot said.

The Turtles and their friends had never met anyone like him before.

"Everyone hold on to something," said Fugitoid as he took control of the spaceship. They zoomed into space!

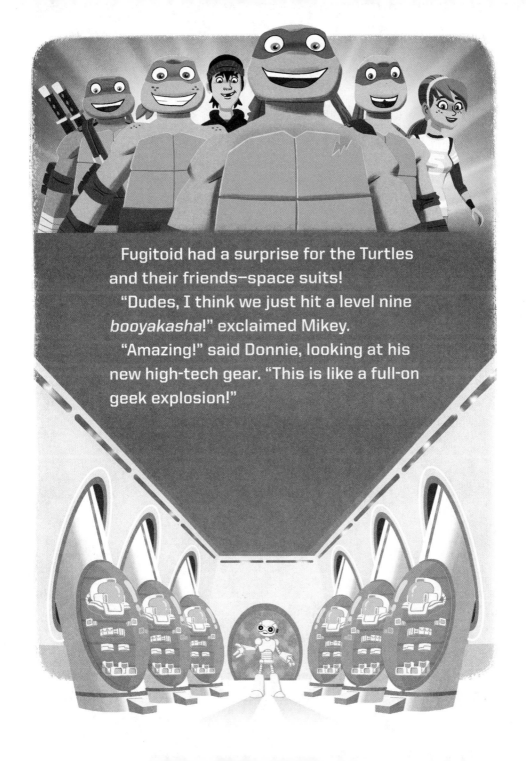

Fugitoid had a surprise for the Turtles and their friends—space suits!

"Dudes, I think we just hit a level nine *booyakasha*!" exclaimed Mikey.

"Amazing!" said Donnie, looking at his new high-tech gear. "This is like a full-on geek explosion!"

The Turtles couldn't wait to take their very first space walk!

"*Cowabungaaaa!*" yelled Mikey, floating through space.

"Why did I think this would be cool?" Raphael said to himself. "Please don't hurl. Please don't hurl."

Meanwhile, Donnie and Fugitoid
noticed space boulders zooming
their way.
"Asteroids!" shouted Donnie.

The team raced back to the ship. Fugitoid
steered the spaceship out of harm's way, but
they needed to refuel.

"What are we gonna do?" asked Donnie.

"Drop by an alien spaceport!" replied Fugitoid.
"There's one right there. Planet Varanon."

"Your computer says this planet is home to space pirates, thieves, and smugglers," said Donnie as he exited the ship.

"I like it already," replied Raphael with a smile.

"Do be careful," warned Fugitoid.

The planet was strange and confusing to the Turtles. Mikey tried to eat a cake, but it turned out to be a creature—with teeth that could bite back!

The Turtles and their friends made enemies everywhere they went.

"Guys, we gotta move right now!" yelled Donnie as angry vendors chased them.

"This way," said April. "Fast!"

As they tried to escape, the team ran right into a big, mean alien.

"Oh, sorry, sir!" said Leo.

"Do not touch me!" replied the fearsome creature. "I should vaporize you all! Do you know who I am?"

"I am Lord Dregg! Ruler of Planet Sectoid and lord of all insect life in the universe," he bragged.

"We've taken way tougher dudes than you," replied Casey. Angrily, Dregg grabbed Casey! "Let him go!" yelled April.

Raphael joined the fight, and Dregg dropped his canister. A strange powder spilled out of it.
"My star spice!" howled Dregg. "That was worth five million zemulaks!"

"Robugs! Attack!" shouted Dregg.

"Get 'em!" yelled Leo.

The battle began!

The Turtles quickly defeated the robugs, but this only angered Dregg.

"You have all made a terrible mistake," he said. "Come to me, Hornetron!"

The Turtles looked up
and saw Hornetron, Dregg's
huge insect-like spacecraft.
    "Start the ship!" yelled Leo.
"We gotta go!"
    The team piled in, and Fugitoid
prepared for takeoff.

Luckily, the Turtles' ship had lasers.
Zip! Zip! Zip! The Turtles blasted all
the robugs . . . or so they thought.

Without warning, a robug broke in to the ship!
Casey Jones used his hockey stick to flick
an explosive photon puck at the robug. "Casey
Jones shoots . . . and scores!" he said.

The defeated robug dropped to
the floor.

"Brilliant!" exclaimed Fugitoid. "Everyone get ready for tachyon warp!"

As their ship zoomed forward, the team watched Dregg's ship fade into the distance.

"Yes! We made it," cheered Leo. Everyone celebrated their escape.

"We got the tools; we got the talent," added Mikey.

The Turtles smiled, but they knew the mission to save Earth from the evil Triceratons had only just begun. . . .